It's Snowing!

Olivier Dunrea

FARRAR STRAUS GIROUX ❄ NEW YORK

The text of this book is set in Bitstream Calligraphic 421.
The illustrations are rendered in gouache on
140 lb. rough D'Arches watercolor paper.

Copyright © 2002 by Olivier Dunrea
All rights reserved
Distributed in Canada by Douglas & McIntyre Ltd.
Color separations by Chroma Graphics PTE Ltd.
Printed and bound in the United States of America by Berryville Graphics
First edition, 2002
10 9 8 7 6 5 4 3 2

Library of Congress Cataloging-in-Publication Data
Dunrea, Olivier.
    It's snowing / Olivier Dunrea.— 1st ed.
        p. cm.
    Summary: A mother shares the magic of a snowy night with her baby.
    ISBN 0-374-39992-1
    [1. Snow—Fiction. 2. Mother and child—Fiction. 3. Babies—Fiction.] I. Title.

PZ7.D922 It 2002
[E]—dc21   00-42172

For Jan, who remembers
a dark, snowy night in West Chester

It's a dark dark,
cold cold night.

Mama rocks the cradle.
The cradle rocks Baby.
Baby softly sleeps.
Mama sighs and nods her head.
Baby sighs and sucks his thumb.

It's a dark dark,
cold cold night.
Mama stirs the fire.
Baby rustles in his sleep.

Mama opens the heavy door.
Snowflakes spatter from the sky.
"It's snowing!" Mama sings.
Baby wakes and blinks.
"Baby, it's snowing!"

Mama bundles Baby
in thick warm furs.
"Baby, it's snowing!"
Baby bounces up and down.

Mama scrunches into her coat.
She ties a long long scarf
around her neck.
She pulls on thick warm mittens.
Mama scoops up Baby
and trundles out the door.

"It's snowing!" Mama sings.
Baby sings along.
"Baby, see the snow!"
Baby squirms in Mama's arms.

"Baby, smell the snow!"
Baby breathes deeply.
"Baby, hear the snow!"
Baby holds his breath.

"Baby, taste the snow!"
Baby opens his mouth.
"Baby, touch the snow!"
Baby flies into the air.

"It's snowing!" Mama sings.
"Let's build a snow troll."
Baby smiles and sneezes.

"It's snowing!" Mama sings.
"Let's sled down the hill."
Baby laughs and squeals.

"It's snowing!" Mama sings.
"Let's ride our ice bear."
Baby wriggles with glee.

"It's snowing," Mama says.
"It's time to go back to bed.
"It's snowing," Mama whispers.
"It's time to rock the cradle."
Baby yawns and nods his head.

Mama rocks the cradle.
The cradle rocks Baby.
Baby softly sleeps.
Mama sighs and nods her head.
Baby sighs and sucks his thumb.

It's a dark dark,
cold cold night.
It's snowing!